This F...ing Fat-Ass Baldheaded Bitch, Thanks You

Halafa Parke

This isn't what I thought my first book would be, but circumstances change things. As women, the word "bitch" is often used to break us down. My doing the right thing does not make me a bitch. A woman being strong and assertive and knowing who she is, is not a bitch. I am guilty of using the word in anger, but there are times when I use it playfully, but most times when it is applied to a woman, there is nothing playful about it.

The title of this book stemmed from being called a fucking fat-ass baldheaded bitch for doing my job, and it was done in a way to break me down. I am happy with myself, and that is the only thing that matters. So, call me a fat ass baldheaded bitch all day long, and I will take it as a compliment. You can't break me down. You have tried and failed. Don't let anyone break you down. Take what they try to use to break you down and show them just how strong you are. As women our roots are planted deep and it takes a lot to uproot us. Enjoy.

Table of Content

This F...ing Fat-Ass Baldheaded Bitch, Thanks You

This f...ing fat-ass baldheaded bitch

This f...ing fat-ass, baldheaded bitch
might not be a size 2, but that doesn't
stop men from seeing the beauty that is me.

This baldheaded bitch might not be your idea of
what a beautiful woman should be, but that is just
your opinion.
Men want me wherever I go, and it is not because of
my looks.

A woman like you, who has nothing to offer the
world besides what you consider your beauty, could
never understand a beauty such as mine.

My beauty is on the outside, yes, but that is not
where I shine. I shine from the inside, where my
love is pure and bright, like a beacon leading others
to me.

My beauty is in my heart, where I love without
reservation. My beauty is in my kindness, where I
give all I have to all I can.

I am loved for my goodness, kindness, respect for
others, and above all, my respect for myself.
You may look down on this baldheaded fat-ass
bitch, but only you and others like you who have no
hope of ever coming close to being the woman I am
or the woman I am destined to become does.

You reveal more about your true self and your future
when you try to break me down with such a phrase.
Instead, you just added one more step on my future
ladder, one you can never climb because the height
is such that your dreams don't reach that far.

You just learned something about this baldheaded,
fat-ass bitch.
I always take what little people like you, insecure
about their place in the world, throw at me and use it
to pave the way to my future.
A future that has endless possibilities.

Halafa Parke

Beautiful just as I am

I never use to be very confident in who I am
I started gaining weight at age twelve,
and children can be so cruel,
and so, can some adults.
I've been called ugly and fat and everything
imaginable in-between, but I will spare you that.
It took me a long time and a world of pain to realize
that I am not here to make everyone else happy.
I am here to make only myself happy.

I see women do such drastic things to look a certain
way and fit into the beauty mold this world says a
woman has to fit to be beautiful; well, that is a lie.
Beauty does come in all shapes, sizes, and shades.

When I look in the mirror, I see all my
imperfections, and if I do anything to cover them
up, it is to make me happy and not everyone else
comfortable, and what I see is the most beautiful
woman in the world staring back at me, and I smile
at her.

We are who we are, and until we learn to love
ourselves for the imperfect person in the mirror
staring back at us, nothing we do on the outside will
ever change our beauty.

Who we are on the inside will always shine through,
no doctor, no cream, nothing can alter the true you,
and the true you are where your beauty is reflected.

Don't ever change yourself to please others.
That just leaves unhappiness shadowing your
footsteps.
You have no peace because you are always trying to
feed the beast.

When you realize you no longer can, you are left
broken and alone, a stranger staring back at you
from your own eyes, and all those who wanted to
change the fundamental you have moved on to their
next victim, and you aren't even a memory.

Moving mountains

I have been through hell, but every time I get
knocked down, I get up stronger than before.
I've been looked down on, called names, I've been
abused, treated differently because of who I am, but
I am strong, forged in fire, and nothing you do will
keep me down.

I am a woman, and we give birth to life, carry the
world on our shoulders, our love brings light to
drive away the darkness.
We have suffered through the worst life has to offer,
yet still, give a smile to help build up others.

You make assumptions about our strength and our
worth, neither of which can be measured.
I am quiet, so you think that says everything there is
to say about me, but underneath the quiet is steel
wrapped in silk.

Nothing you do can stop my progress.
My determination is a mountain you can't climb.
The faith I have in myself you can't begin to
understand.
You climb walls, but I move mountains.
You see the end of the road; I see the beginning of
an adventure.
The road of life is never smooth, and sometimes the
path is through the mountains.

I can't afford to be afraid of the dark, but be prepared to fight the enemies hiding in its midst. I can't let what you think about me affect what I know to be true, affect who I know I am for sure. Your negative opinion has no place in my life, no effect on my dreams; instead, it provides the fuel that drives my future.

Halafa Parke

I am a woman

I am a woman,
a very foxy lady,
I am sexy yet shy,
I am loving and proud,
I am intelligent, almost brilliant.
I am a woman.
A courageous woman is what I am.
I am free to do what I want,
to be all I can be, for
I am a woman and proud.

There's almost nothing in this world I can't do, and
nowhere I cannot go.
I'm always willing and ready for anything.
I am strong and mighty.
I'm funny with a sense of intelligence.
I am a teacher and a student.
I am a woman and proud.

When I walk down the street, all eyes are
on me cause I'm naturally beautiful.
When I walk into a room, you wonder
about the sudden silence.
Men are intimidated by my brilliance and others by
my beauty.
I am not afraid to live and be.
I'm not trying to be who I am not.
I live up to my own standards because I am me.
A woman and proud.

I know who I am and where I am going.
I know where I have been and how far I've come. I
work hard for what I have.
I fight for what I believe.
I'm not ashamed of who I am.
Who am I? A woman, that's who!
I am the strength of all the women
who are afraid to fight and fear to all
men who are afraid of the dark.
I am a woman, a courageous woman, and proud.

Halafa Parke

Ways of the world

A man is considered weak and a fool if he cries;
feminine for a woman.
A man should be brave, strong, and
courageous at all times. So, it is written.

A woman should be meek,
loving, with her tender touch,
and her care of others, for that
is the way of the world.

But fool is the man who does not cry,
and shame on a woman who is not strong,
for a man could never be without a woman,
and a woman could never survive a
man without being strong.

The portrait of a woman

The portrait of a woman
beauty and elegance;
fragility and strength;
intelligence and pride;
kind and caring.

The touch of her hand,
the sway of her hips,
the smile on her lips,
the fire in her eyes,
the power of her hate,
the magnificence of her love.
To hear her laugh, you'd give
your soul to touch her lips.

The portrait of a woman
she laughs, she cries,
she is a sister and a friend,
a mother, and a daughter.

She gives with everything or takes it all.
Try to understand a woman, and
you will be lost forever.

Love her as you should, and
she will always be there for you.
The gentleness of her voice,
the harsh reality of her world.

A woman's eyes are the way to her soul.

Halafa Parke

A woman's heart is the path to untold joy.
The portrait of a woman, untouchable.

If I were beautiful

Would you love me if, somehow, I was beautiful?
Would you acknowledge the love all can see shining
from me?
Would you appreciate all the things I do for you, big
and small?

If I were beautiful, would you show me the world?
Would you shower me in diamonds?
Would you dress me like a queen?

If I were beautiful, would you laugh at
the games I play,
brush away my ignorance,
be so overcome by this beauty that you
tolerate my greed?

If I were beautiful, would we be friends,
would we be lovers? Tell me,
would you make me your wife?

If I were beautiful, would you stand by me no matter
the cost?
Would you profess your love for me, turn away from
anyone who warns you about me?
Would you die for me forsaking the truth that you
know?

I'm not beautiful, so you look through me.
I'm not beautiful, so you know not my name.
You see me every day but know not my face.

Halafa Parke

I'm not beautiful, according to you;
so, who am I?
If I was your definition of beautiful, would you
know my name, know my face?
Would you call my name?
Would I give a damn?

What a woman sees in herself

What a man sees in a woman
is not what she sees in herself.

A man is looking for beauty in face and in form; a
woman's beauty is natural and honest, and it shines
from deep within.

A woman's beauty is in the way she walks,
the sway of her hips, sexy and oh, so appealing.

It's in the way she laughs full and bold
and not afraid to shine.

Her beauty is in the way she loves with her whole
heart, giving it everything she has.

It's in the way she speaks, the way she acts,
like a woman, like the lady she is.

It's in the clothes she wears.
It's in the things she says.
A woman's beauty comes full circle when she loves;
when she gives life, the light that shines from her is
almost blinding in its purity.

It's in her friendship, her loyalty;
it's in the love and care she showers on
those around her, asking only to be loved in return.

What I am looking for

They say hi, tell me about your friend.
I used to be surprised, but I am no more.
I used to be hurt, but now I just brush them off, for
they are not what I am looking for.

We became friends, or so I thought;
he just wants to be closer to her.
I told him to get out of my life,
we were friends no more; it didn't
hurt as much as it should, for
he was not what I was looking for.

Tall, dark, and handsome in his case
was not a cliché, with deep-brown eyes,
he warmed me to my soul.
His laughter flowed over me like warm
honey, the comfort of his arms, the safest
place my heart has ever known.
With intelligence shining in his eyes as
he makes me laugh, mischief dancing in his heart as I
fall in love with him.
Finally, this is the man I have been looking for.

Know when to leave the boys behind

It makes me sad, and I have to shake my head when
I see women fighting each other over a man,
breaking each other down, and building up his ego.
Giving up her power as a woman, losing faith in her
strength to stand on her own and prove to him she
is better off without him in her life.
Because what he is, is a dead weight dragging her
down and keeping her from realizing her greatness.

As women, we are the prize, and a man should fight
for the right to have us in their life.
A man should work hard to make sure we are happy,
and we will do the same for him.
Worship the ground we walk on, and we will let
them see why they do.
A man who deserves our love will respect that love,
and he will cherish us.
He will give his life to protect us and make sure no
one, not even ourselves, does anything to cause us
harm because that is what we deserve.
That is what we are worth.
A real man will know this.

Women who break each other down do this because
they deal with boys and do not associate with men.
A man knows a woman's worth and thus respects
her and her place in his life.
I refuse to sell myself short and fight over someone
not deserving of my time, let alone my love.

Halafa Parke

Some women need to know their worth, know when
it is time to leave the boys behind to play with their
toys and find a man to help build a future, to help
make life.

I will never be that woman

I will never be that woman who doesn't love herself enough to live her own life.
I will never be that woman who makes her choices based on what pleases the man in her life.
I have my own mind, make my own money, so I live my own life on my own terms.
If he loves me, he will support me.
He will want the best for me, the best for us, not what is best for him.
He will be my support system, just as I am his because we are a team.

Some women are so insecure about who they are that they don't know how to live without a man.
Become so dependent on him they lose themselves.
Who then do they become but a shadow, an empty vessel?
You like what he likes. You want what he wants.
You have no say. Your voice lost along the way.

I am a woman who needs to know who I am.
I have to love who I am before I can love anyone else.
If I lose myself in him, then how do I give my best to him? Who is he loving?
Because it is not me if I am lost in him?
I want a man that respects my choices and supports my dreams. My success is our success, and my failures are our failures.

Halafa Parke

Every woman needs to know who she is and her
place in the world.
She should be encouraged and supported to reach
for the stars, not be a shadow of a man who does
not deserve her love or her devotion.

I am worth more

He came with roses to say I'm sorry,
champagne to make me mellow,
and chocolate-covered strawberries
because he knows that's what I like.
He said I'm sorry, and my lips formed a pout.
He kissed me here. He kissed me there,
trying to break me down.
I fell into him, loving how he makes me feel.
I felt his smile against my skin.
I pushed away from him; not this time,
I said to him.
I am worth more than you give, and I value myself
too much to settle for less than I deserve.
If you are not man enough to stand up with a strong
woman like me and treat me the way I should be
treated, then you don't need to be in my life, and
most definitely not in my bed.
I can find a man who will value me and treat me like
the queen I am. You are playing the
games of a boy, and what I need is a man.
If you are not up to the challenge, the door is behind
you. You know the way out.

Halafa Parke

Raped

Fear, such fear, I felt his hand over my mouth,
squeezing my soul, tearing at my clothes as he tried
to get to my most private self.

Tears came from this place that would be
lost inside me, I felt him push into my body
as I screamed at this invasion of my most inner self.

I was lost in a moment, never to find my way again.
He took from me what was mine to give, took more
than he ever knew: my ability to trust again.
I look in the mirror but can no longer see myself.

Where there once was light is now
pure darkness, and in this darkness lives my greatest
fear.

I wonder how it is not to live in fear.
How does it feel to live in skin that doesn't cry out
to be ripped from my bones,
where my soul doesn't scream for justice of this
thief, who comes in the dark, all my dreams stolen
by this stealer of souls, this rapist of my body?

I want to tell your story

I want to tell your story and
expose your pain to the world.
I want them to see your soul and
ask themselves, could I live that?
I want them to see your smile and
say how brave, hear you laugh, and
have tears come to their eyes.
I want to tell your story.

I want to tell your story and
invite the world into your bed,
have them be there when you look
in the mirror and see what you see,
have a memory, and feel the pain you feel.
I want you to go for a walk and have them
ask, where do you find the strength?
See you cry and ask where your courage has gone?
I want to tell your story.

I want to tell your story and
invite them into your day.
Have you pour them tea and ask them to sit.
I want them to look at you with wonder
in their eyes at your gentle ways.
I want them to envy the peace you have
found at such a dreadful cost.
I want them to listen to your words and wish to
trade places.
I want them to want to be you, but ask themselves if
they could have made it this far.

Halafa Parke

I want them to want you dead, even as they fall in
love with you.
I want to tell your story.

You hit me

The promise of life was so vivid before me,
the demise of love so powerful,
the awakening of hate so complete.
The cycle unbroken, you appeared before me.

The wind off the sea, a howl ripped from my chest,
the sky was blue, the day was new, my pain
intensified, and therein my journey began.

The very first time I turned away,
I made excuses.
But soon after, I began to die.
No more did that light shine from my eyes.
No more did my laughter brings joy
to those around me.
No more could I find my soul walking around with
no direction, no will of my own, you dictating my
every move.

I was no longer a leader but a helpless follower.
After one so many times, I died.
And when I awoke, I could hurt no more.
My hurt had helped me to heal, and you,
you could hurt me no more.

Only myself to blame

I knew the type of man he was when we met.
He was upfront about who he was and what he
wanted from me, so I can't say I wasn't warned or
that I didn't get into this with my eyes wide open.
And that makes the pain even harder to bear.

I have never before let my guard down where a man
is concerned.
Too bad I didn't take the same approach this time
around.

I knew what the outcome would be if I went
forward and that it wouldn't be what I need or what
I could handle, but for the first time in what seems
like a lifetime, I wanted the forbidden.

He kissed me that first night, and for days
it was all I thought about.
I wanted to taste his lips again and so much more.
I wanted the memory of being in his arms.
I wanted to know how it felt to be loved by this
man.
I wanted him to make me feel things I never felt
before.

What he made me feel was an emptiness I never felt
before.
I knew I shouldn't have, but I gave him the best of
me, and now I've lost a part of myself I will never
get back.

He was honest with me from the moment we met, so now I have only myself to blame.

Halafa Parke

All you had to do was see me

I have a question for you, what would you say if I
told you I didn't love you?
Would you call me a fool for not knowing the real
thing or be relieved you won't hurt my feelings when
you walk out on me?

How wrong was I to think that you would come to
care even a little about me after so long together.
But I won't cry, not for something that was never
real.

You will never know how much you have hurt me,
but one day, you will realize how much you just lost.

I gave you more than anyone ever has
but you just couldn't see it.
I can't keep on loving you when you don't know
what love is.
I can't open myself up for any more pain, for any
more loss.

I know you have never felt love,
never known true tenderness before,
but all you had to do was look into my eyes,
concentrate on my touch, listen to the tone of my
voice.
It was all there freely given, but you were too blind
to see the love that was real.

If I loved you

Who would I be if you loved me?
Would I be beautiful and elegant or just plain me?
The woman who makes you smile,
whose laughter you can't live without,
whose touch your body craves night and day.

Who would I be if you loved me?
Would I be rich and famous or just plain me?
The woman who makes the sun shine brighter, who
brings the rain so life will prosper, whose touch can
soothe your burning temper.

Who would I be if you loved me?
Would I be a temptress and a tease or just plain me?
The woman who loves you with all she's got, who
brings joy to your life,
whose passion for you knows no end.

Who would you be if I loved you?
More blessed than any man has a right to be, with all
my love showered on thee,
and a passion that burns hotter than the sun;
you would be the only man I see.

Halafa Parke

Finding myself

I am finally on my way,
on my way to a better tomorrow,
on my way to a bigger dream.
The sun is shining brighter and
my laughter flowing free.
I finally found within me the
strength to put forth the very best of me.
No more I can't, no more I don't know,
now it's I will, I won't falter.
The world is waiting for me to take hold and never
let go, to show them what I can do, who I can be,
for my strength lies within where I can only grow
stronger, where my will, will push me further.
I am so much more than my dreams
more than the person you see.

Am I? I am

Am I nothing more, nothing less than just a woman?
Aren't I a mother?
A daughter?
A sister?
A teacher and a friend?

Am I nothing more, nothing less than just the apple
of someone's eyes?
Aren't I the tree on which the apple grows?
Free to live and die whenever I please?

Am I nothing more, nothing less than a laborer of
love?
Can't I sin?
Can't I hate?
Can't I forgive and forget?

I am a lot more but nothing less than a woman, the
apple of someone's eyes
and a laborer of love.
I am a woman who loves.

Halafa Parke

I am going to show them who I am

Being different is never easy.
People look at me like I don't belong.
Being who I am have always been hard,
but I won't let anyone take away my dignity
because pride is all, I have.

I'm going to show them who I am.
I'm going to show them how strong I am.
I'm going to show them beauty
isn't all we need; that the strength
inside will carry me farther.

I won't let them break me down.
When they laugh, I'll laugh with them.
And even if I cry, they won't see my
tears fall. Fools they are.
They think they do me wrong.
They don't know they give me all I need to succeed;
they don't know they are the way to my dreams.

I'm going to show them who I am,
I'm going to show them what life is all about, that
supposed beauty isn't what makes the world goes
'round, and that the strength I have inside will take
me all the way.

People assume they know me.
When they don't know what I'm about.
What they see is not who I am.
Who I am is someone they'll never understand.

This F…ing Fat-Ass Baldheaded Bitch, Thanks You

Who I am is more than they could ever hope to be.

I am going to show them who I am.
I'll make sure they understand,
what they think just might be wrong,
and when they see me, they won't know
I'm the one they thought they knew.
I'm going to show them who I am.

Walking away

I knew a man once,
a man I could have loved.
He was kind, and he was brave,
he was troubled, but he had his ways.

He showed me his heart and made me want to heal;
he pushed me away, but I held on tighter.
He was my way when I didn't know I was lost.
He had his strengths I could embrace.

Through the dark, I held his hand,
in the light, he pulled away.
I could have been the one for him;
I could have given him what he needs.

He could do without my love,
he could do without me.
I pulled away. It broke my heart.
He looked away. I broke down and cried.

He was a man I could have loved.
I became the woman he could never have.
I will be strong. I will make it on my own.
He held out his hand to me.
The hardest thing I ever did,
I turned and walked away.

I cried

Do you want to know the honest truth?
I cried when you let me go.
When you let me walk out of your life,
I cried for the fool you are and the love that I feel.
I cried because maybe I wasn't strong enough
because maybe I wasn't woman enough.

To be everything to each other and have it end to
know a person so well, his touch,
his smile, the sound of his walk.
To have tasted his tears and his joy,
to watch him sleep and fall in love all over again, to
become so old and yet so new to each other.

I have cried tears because I miss the closeness we
shared, the joy we found in the little things.
The way you hold me when the rain is falling, the
way you love me to the very end.

I cry because I miss your smile, the awful sound of
your laugh.
You gave me strength and so much more.
You filled up all the empty spaces in my life like
nothing or no one ever has.
I cried because fool I am, I know I will love you
forever, just as I know you will love me.

Would that the world was not such a cruel place.
I wish that we could love the way we wanted.

Halafa Parke

I cry for this love that holds so tight to my heart. I cry because of the hunger that lingers in my body for your touch, the need my soul has to be one with yours.

I cry because we both know this can never be more than it is right now, for though we love each other, we both go home to someone else.
Anger surrounds me, loneliness enfolds me, and the tears keep falling as I cry.

Through it all

We have been friends for so long,
longer than I've known anyone else.
You have held me through loss and the pain it
brought.
You've been there through love that only broke my
heart.
You have seen me at my worst, known me at my
best.
You have seen me cry. You've made me laugh.
You're the one I call in good times and bad,
I can count on you for the truth,
even if it's not what I want to hear.
Your arms are my shelter,
your smile, my guide.
I never knew it was in me to care so
much for another person,
but when you hurt, I hurt.
I can't stand to see the sadness
in your eyes and know there is
nothing I can do to make you smile.
You are home for me, the only safe place I've ever
known;
you lend me wisdom so I can be proud.
You give me laughter so my heart can be free.
Know that you can count on me to be there through
it all.
I will be what you have always been for me, your
shelter, your safe place.

Halafa Parke

No matter how dark the night, I will be your light.
I'll lend you a shoulder if you need to cry, be there to
listen when you are ready to talk.
We are in this together.
Even if the world turns its back, I'll always stand by
your side through it all.
I will be with you like you have always been there for
me.

When he asked me to marry him

We have been together for a long time;
no one thought we would make it this far.
I wasn't good enough for him, they would say, yet,
he never turned me away.

You don't find many men like him anymore.
He doesn't go around trying to sleep with
every female he meets.
He is devoted to me, and I am secure in the love I
know he feels.
He is my best friend, and I am his, so when he asked
me to marry him, of course, my answer was yes.

At that moment, the world was created just for the
two of us; that moment he was giving me, a moment
when all my dreams were coming true.
I could see his love for me shining through the tears
in his eyes.

I felt joy rush through me like a flash of light, and I
knew this was meant to be.
He is like no man I have ever known, like no man in
this world.
And what I felt for him is like nothing any woman
has ever felt before.

Trusting my heart again

It's hard to trust again when it's your heart that was
betrayed.
To find it in yourself to open that door ever again
and give another even the tiniest glimpse inside.
Remembering how much of myself I had given,
what a fool to believe all the things he said,
all the promises he made.
He spoon-fed me lies, and my heart had no chance
against the smoothness of it all.

It's hard putting the pieces back,
rebuilding one's self with armor around your heart.
A good man comes along, but it is hard to look
beyond his smile to acknowledge the pull you feel
when he's near, to let go of the hurt and pain, and
maybe love again.
How do I take the first step and risk my heart again
when I don't know if I can trust what it is I feel?
When I don't know if I can trust my heart?

Stronger together

Some women say they can make it on their own they
don't need a man.
They say I pay my own bills and I can buy whatever
I want.
I don't want a man in my life to pay my bills, and I
can make it on my own because I make my own
money.
I need a man in my life because I am a woman, and
God made man to be the other half of me.

I want him for his smiles and his kisses;
I want him for the solid strength he is when I stand
with my back to his chest, the warmth of his body
keeping me safe.
I need a man in my life to hold me when I am
falling, to help lift me up when the world breaks me
down.
The love and support of a real man are priceless, a
man who cherishes me because he respects and
loves me.
He is a man who wants only me and leaves skirt-
chasing to the boys.

A man who brings me flowers and gifts because they
would brighten my day; a man who will let me stand
on his shoulders to see over the crowd.
A man who is my best friend, and I am his.
He doesn't leave me behind to hang out with his
friends, but I am woman enough to let him out of
my sight because I know he will be faithful to me.

Halafa Parke

I know my worth, and so does he.
I am priceless to him, just as he is to me.
I don't need a man for what he can do for me,
I need a man for the love I know we can share,
for the dream, we can build.
I need a man because together, I know we are
stronger.

The man of my dreams

The man of my dreams
the fire in his eyes
the depth of his pain
the naughty things he whispers
the wicked things he does, the way I feel.
He pushes me away
he hides his heart from me
so afraid that I will hurt him.
If only he would look into my eyes
and see my own fears.

I love to touch him
I love his scent
the feel of his body against mine,
the way he kisses, I feel them in my soul.
I love the feeling of his hand knowing me,
loving me.
I love gazing into his deep-brown eyes,
the sometimes laziness of his touch.
How complete I feel in those moments.

But loving him is not easy as he pushes me away
I wish I had the key to unlock his heart
and soothe away the pain keeping him captive
I wish my touch alone could free him to love,
to feel again, to know that love is real and can be
faithful.

Why do you like me?

Why do you like me?
Why do you really like me?
I am not very kind to you, saying things that would
piss off any other man.
I don't encourage you, give the slightest clue I'd ever
go out with you, yet you are always around, always
smiling, laughing, and saving me from myself and
from the world.
Don't you ever get frustrated and just want to leave,
to say the hell with you, you are not worth my time,
and walk away?

Why do you like me?
I see pretty girls and the way they look at you.
I see the other guys and the way they look at me.
Yet, here you are day after day, hanging around me.
Don't you care about the way I treat you, the things I
say to you, how little I appreciate all you do for me?

Why do you like me?
I know why I am starting to like you
even though I don't want to.
You're different from other men I've come across.
You care. You aren't put off by any of the things I
do.
You encourage me to be who I am.
You stand up to me, stand by me
right or wrong, your business or not
you tell me like it is.
I know why I like you. I just wish

This F…ing Fat-Ass Baldheaded Bitch, Thanks You

I could figure out why you like me.

Halafa Parke

Why I like you

Why do I like you?
I like you because you are different from any woman
I've ever known.
You say and do the things you do
to hide your pain, to not get hurt again.
I smile and laugh when I am around you
because, in you, I have found my home.
I save you from yourself because you save me as
well.
I don't get frustrated and leave because I see beyond
your pain to see to the heart of you.

I like you because you are a woman and
you are right.
They are girls, and they don't know
who they are and what they want, and
those guys don't see you because they are boys who
cannot see your beauty.
They cannot appreciate your strength.
I know how you treat me now, but I also know how
you will treat me when you realize what is already in
your heart.
Everything I do for you now is building the
foundation for our future.

I don't only like you; I am in love with you.
I have spent a lifetime searching the world for you,
and nothing you do will push me away.
Your strength in the midst of your pain humbles me.

You don't play the games some women do with the men in their lives where they use a man and move on.
You are a woman looking for more.
 I know you will stand up to me even as you stand by me.
You will tell me the truth and build me up.
You are a strong, beautiful woman, and that is what I like about you.
That is what I want in my life.

Tomorrow

It looks to be a beautiful day,
but looks can be deceiving
because it's ever so cold outside.
I wonder what tomorrow has in store
for me, wisdom to make the right choices
knowledge to understand, courage
to see it through?

I wonder what tomorrow has in store
for me, love to mend my broken heart,
strength to make it through the day
fear to keep the pain away?

I wonder what tomorrow has in store for me,
misery to bring me low, laughter to
brighten my day, weakness to lead me astray?

I wonder what tomorrow has in store for me.
I look outside. The sun is shining. It looks to be a
beautiful day, but looks can be
deceiving because it's ever so cold out there.

A memory of love

The day was cold when we met,
the fire in your eyes warmed me,
the strength in your arms comforted me,
the taste of your kiss filled me.

My memories are pure and sweet,
clean as the morning air.
I embrace the time we had while
letting go of the past.
I loved you like I loved no one else.
The memory of your love seems like a dream
yet it seems as if I could reach out and touch it,
reach out and touch you.

When love catches hold, it never lets you go.
It makes you reach for the sky and
more often than not, we do make it
the memory of our love will always be
with me, be a part of me, even as I let you go.

Halafa Parke

Between you and me

I have loved, and I have lost.
I have lived and almost died.
I like what I like, and there
is no changing my mind.
I don't like games, so you might
as well say what is on your mind.
I will be honest at all times so
if I don't like something, then
that's what I will say.
I'm not trying to push you away.
I'm telling you upfront who I am.
If you don't want to stay,
let me show you the door,
but if you know what you want,
and you've heard what I said, maybe
this could be between you and me.

Learning to love again

I have been down this road before,
loving where love did not love me in return.
I cannot give all of me again, and I want to let you
in, into my heart, into my soul, into my body, but do
you deserve all of me?

I have felt the sting of betrayal.
It left a bitter taste on my tongue.
It was such a fight to get back to a place where I
could trust myself and let anyone into my heart
again.
It was a journey to loving again, but you found a way
to open the door of my heart.

I pray I am making the right choice letting you in
because I love you like I never knew I could.
I love you in a way I never wanted to.
You fill my heart. You're in my soul.
You gave me hope for a new future.

You made me love when I didn't think I could again,
not in this lifetime.
Baby, what if this isn't real?
I am scared I feel too much.
I want to touch what I cannot see.
I watch you sleep as the doubts creep in
But, baby, for you, I am willing to love again.

Halafa Parke

Silent tears

I hear the talk,
I hear the laugh,
and silent tears run down my face.

I see the looks,
feel your disgust,
and silent tears run down my face.

For once, I wish to be beautiful for you to see. For
once, I want to be someone else in your eyes, and
silent tears run down my face.

I hold my head down to avoid the looks,
but can I avoid the jeers?
And silent tears run down my face.

I want to cry for you to see,
but I won't give you that part of me.
I want to laugh, but my laughter is trapped inside.

I can't run away from who I am. I've tried.
You make me doubt myself,
you make me hate me,
yet I can't return the favor in kind,
and silent tears run down my face into
my heart, my soul, and I explode, tears
flowing everywhere as I cry.

I wither to an empty shell, the shell
of who I am, of what I am, and I have

you, the people of the world, to thank for that, I cry
a bit more until nothing is left of me, nothing more
to give, nothing more to feel, just a shadow of who I
used to be wandering around, trying to find a place
where I belong, and silent tears run down my face.

Halafa Parke

Same as you

Life would be so much easier if I
could lock the world out.
I am tired of being strong and brave;
I just want to be normal.

So, I have a limp. Is that cause for you to stare?
So, I'm not as skinny as you.
What do you care?
My eyes are crossed.
What do you want me to do, set them straight?

When I was born, I wasn't a perfect baby.
Should I have died?
So, I'm not able to learn as fast as you.
Should I stop trying to be a success?
So, I look different. Don't tell me you want me to
look like you.

You can stare all you want, but I won't go away, and
I won't apologize for who I am.
I refuse to give in to your vanity.
Perfect, I may not be, but strong I am,
stronger than even you because I have to be, for
each day, just by being alive, I prove
that I deserve to be here the same as you.

Violated

He kisses me and tells me he loves me.
He tells me he loves me and touches my breast.
He tells me he loves me as he lifts my blouse over
my chest.
He tells me he loves me and wants to make love to
me, me! Who would ever think a guy like him would
want a girl like me?
He makes me laugh, and I feel beautiful and so
special when I am with him.
I wake up, and I'm on a cloud. I fall in love again
every time I see his beautiful face.
His love for me is something to see, and I think I'm
ready to show him my love for him.
I could see the look on his face, almost triumphant,
as he laid me down.

Lifting my dress, he told me he loved me.
I felt unsure, uncomfortable, but I wanted to make
him happy, and I was happy knowing he was it,
knowing he was the one.
It was as if he slapped me in the face the way he
acted when I saw him later.
He walked by me as if we hadn't spent these many
weeks getting to know each other.
His friends, they point and laugh, and I try not to
run away crying; there is my pride.
I saw him kissing another girl. She was beautiful,
nothing like me, and I felt my heart shatter inside of
me, the fool I was.

Halafa Parke

I thought he cared for me, him always telling me he
loves me, and I believed it all.
I felt shame for my actions but knew I'd never let
this happen again.
I'd never be such a fool again, never believe the lies
told to get what someone else wanted.

Telling me what you think I want to hear

Tell me again how much you love me
and want me to love you back.
Tell me how you need me
and wish I needed you too.
Explain again how empty your life is without me.
Tell me how your world would be complete
with me in your arms, show me how precious
love is and how wonderful it can be between you
and me.
Show me how touching can heal even the most
jaded heart
let me see how laughter can soothe an aching soul.
I laugh. Tell me what you think I want to hear.

I gave you so much of myself there was almost
nothing left for me.
Tell me why I should listen to a word you have to
say after all you took why should I give you the time
of day.
All the times you treated me like less than I was and
now that I have moved on and found someone who
treats me right and you realize what you have lost,
now you say the things I longed to hear, now you
want to treat me like you care.

It's funny the power a woman realizes she holds
when she finds out she deserves more.
She no longer puts up with bullshit or allows boys
playing at being men anywhere within her sphere.
You didn't know the gift you had in me,

a woman who stood by you through every storm
that came your way.
You didn't realize the blessing when I would pick
you up and help you put the pieces back together.

Through our relationship, I always put you first but
never once did you concern yourself about my
needs.
I have a man who thinks I can do no wrong
he loves me without question and make sure I want
for nothing, least of all his love and respect.
I was a fool before putting your needs ahead of my
own I would be an even bigger fool to walk away
from true love to come back to someone who knows
nothing of loving someone else.

☐

The Struggle

I was born of a woman and a man
I am flesh and blood to my soul
I make mistakes; I'm human that way.
I cry when I can no longer keep the pain at bay
I love because it's built-in me
I'll have no part of hate. It was never instilled in me.

I face challenges, but I push on through
the struggles only serve to make me stronger.
They say I'm weak because I'm a woman,
yet no man I know could carry my load.
I've laughed in the face of the storm,
pushed back against the waves trying to take me
under.

I have to be stronger because of the world in which
we live.
I have to work harder because I'm coming from
behind.
I have to be smarter because the odds are against
me, many would see me falter, but my determination
and drive know no end.
I find strength in every slight, power in all their
doubts.

Being a woman, I was not made to be broken
but to carry the world on my shoulders.

Halafa Parke

Steel rods run through my spine, and my feet are
rooted to the earth because I'm planted by the
master, watered to grow out of everyone's sight.
There is no end to what I can accomplish
I dream bigger because my world is so small
and nothing will stand in the way of my dreams.
☐

Done waiting for you

I am here on a Saturday night
trying not to think about you but
you are all that I can think about.
I am wondering where you are
and what you are doing.
Do you have someone new and
am I yesterday's news?
I haven't seen you in days
you don't call, you don't come by
and when I call you don't answer.
I know I have no hold on you but
I thought we were starting to build a relationship
and I can't do it by myself.
It takes more than me alone
I am tired of wondering where you are and
hoping you will call, rushing to the phone
each time it rings, praying you're on the line.
If there is someone else, tell me, and
don't just come around when everyone
else is all tied up.
I have better things to do with my time and
my life and none of it includes waiting around for
you.

I love you, but I don't need you

I want you, and I love you, but I don't need you.
I need air to breathe, food to eat, and the lord to
sustain my soul.
People come, and people go. I have no hold on you
if you want to leave. I'll show you the door.
I am strong.
I don't have a problem being on my own.
Being alone, I enjoy being able to
hear my own thoughts.
Yes, I love how you make me smile and
how I feel when I am in your arms,
but my peace of mind, my sense of self, is more
important than being in your arms.
No matter how much I want to, I cannot love you
more than I love myself.
I cannot put your wants ahead of my needs.
You don't love me enough, so I have to love myself
for the both of us.
I won't let you make me feel bad for putting myself
first because that is what I deserve.

I will never forgive you

It matters not to me what you
say or what you do.
Who you love or who you hate,
But when you are alone, remember
you're the one who forgot about me.
Remember you threw my love away
ripped my heart from my body and
said you never loved me.
I cried tears of pain over my lost
but I picked myself up and went on,
without you.

It matters not who you are
or use to be to me.
Not the changes in you
not the promise I see.
For once, I would have done
anything for you
given you my love
my life, but now,
now I am stronger and wiser.
Yes, I still love you bit I will
never forgive you.
☐
☐

Pain

I woke up in tears,
doubled over as if someone
had just served me a blow.
I wanted to die
I wanted out of my skin.
It follows me where ever I go
it creeps up my stomach
at times lodges in my chest,
and vibrates through my body.

I run away, but where to go?
It's everywhere.
Death seems the only way out
it slices through me like a knife on a mission,
hammers in my brain like a woodpecker in a tree.

It's my greatest enemy
my best friend
this pain of mine
it knows no bound
have no time difference
yet I carry it always
nurse it as I would a babe at my breast,
yet I wish to be free from it.

Tears stream down my face
I laugh a bitter sound it may be,
it sounds sweet to my ears.
The agony in my body is driving me mad.
This pain that I'm in love with

This F…ing Fat-Ass Baldheaded Bitch, Thanks You

will see me to my grave.

Halafa Parke

Where do I belong

Where do I belong?
In your arms with all the love you
have to offer,
with all the laughter in your heart,
all the joy in your life.

Where do I belong?
Upon a pedestal with people falling at my feet,
offers so bountiful being given onto me,
all their love that knows no bounds.

Where do I belong?
Up in heaven with angels at my feet,
clouds shaped like hearts and
the devil in disgrace.

Where do I belong?
On a mountain made of gold,
bread made of silver,
wine out of diamonds.

Where do I belong?
On a bed made of flowers,
shoe made of life,
a gown made of fear,
tell me, where do I belong?

Troubled world

I see so much in the world that troubles me.
Things would be so much better if we focused on
how alike we are instead of the differences that stand
in our way.

We are different, but that is what makes us beautiful.
That is what makes us unique and gives us a bridge
to form relationships.
If we took a moment to talk to a stranger, we would
see we are so much more alike than we are different.

We would see that our differences are on the outside
and not in who we are where it counts.
We were not born to hate but taught to hate.
Love is natural, but hate takes so much work.
If only we would learn to embrace our differences
and celebrate being alive instead of hating each other
for things we cannot change, things that aren't meant
to change.

We hurt each other out of ignorance and refuse to
change for the same reason.
The seasons change, and we are all the better for it.
Night turns today, and the sun drives the cold away.
We live in a past we did not create and walk in a
future we refuse to embrace.

They say learn from the past so as not to repeat it,
yet we see the past take more of today every day.

Halafa Parke

Our strength is diminished by our refusal to step
into the present
to accept that we are equals and all deserving of
respect and dignity.
We all deserve the opportunity to be who we are and
to embrace our true destiny.

Wave

I was born in a day
I lived in a year
on a wave headed for heaven
the land wild and free surrounds me.
The wind on my face
a blend of melodies in my ears
wildflowers abloom,
my heart filled with joy.
I was free to enjoy life as
it was before me.
I was destined to be wild
like a herd of buffalos
I was to be great,
I was to be loved,
I was the wave.

I took the wave headed for the sea
I plunged to the bottom of the ocean
and swam a thousand miles,
climbed the highest mountain I did,
overcame my greatest fear.

On the wave headed north, I
jumped on. It was out of control.
Going too fast to hold on, but held on
I did, and at the end of this wave, I
found my way home, to travel another
wave, one calm but still a long way to go.

Halafa Parke

Foolish me

This ever-foolish heart of mine
loving where love will not love me back.
Wanting something that will never be mine,
hoping against hope, me, always the fool.
I wonder if he knew would he laugh
and say how sad.
How many times must I walk this road
before I learn my lesson?
How many tears will I cry?
How much hurt will I endure?
Living in a dream world,
wanting what will never be,
loving a man who will never love me back?

Not today then tomorrow

Today might not be for me,
but I won't give up on tomorrow.
I am clouded in darkness today, but
tomorrow the light will find me.
I may be quiet. Don't mistake that for weakness.

If I don't say don't assume, I don't know.
You make me so angry,
I gain strength from that anger.
You do me wrong; that only makes me
work harder to prove that I am better than you think
I am, smarter than you know.

You talk to me. You laugh with me,
but do I know you?
I could say what you see is what you get,
and deceive you because I know you would believe
me, but there is so much more if you took the time
to look, to see what there is to me.

Halafa Parke

My own

If it was cold outside that night
I could not tell, and I guess all my
mother remembered was the searing
pain that was giving birth, the foul
words I know must have passed through
her lips and my father's fear that if she
could get her hands on him in her pain
she was sure to kill him for putting
her through this yet at the same time he
fervently swears never to put her through
this again.
But all is forgotten when this tiny,
perfect little person is placed in her
arms and its first cries reach her ears.
Its tiny fingers curl around one of hers
while it sucks life's milk from her breast.
The pleasure she feels, the love she can't
explain the joy that overcame her,
her child to love, the one she called
my own.

I see you

What does the world see when they look at you?
What I see is beyond compare.
I see your eyes shining like a million stars.
I see you accepting me, even with all my faults.
I see a heart so big, so open, nothing in the world
comes close.
I see mischief. I hear laughter.
I see you making my world a better place.
I see such beauty.
I'm thankful knowing you love me.
I rejoice in knowing you are a part of me.
No one sees your beauty, but it is blinding to me.
I see grace and compassion.
I see giving and acceptance.
I see love and understanding.
I see that love is a treasure when loving you, and
your smile is a blessing shining down on me.
Each day with you is a gift of untold worth, and
nothing in this world will ever come close to the love
I feel for you. I name it, I claim it, I will never give
you up. You are simply the only one I see.

Halafa Parke

Revenge

Frozen teardrops,
empty dreams,
tomorrow's mystery,
yesterday is best forgotten,
the emptiness inside,
sadness,
loneliness,
anger unleashed,
forgiveness,
live for the moment,
forget yesterday,
tomorrow belongs to no man,
cut your path in life,
build dreams upon hope, and
upon hope, you build life.
Listen to none but the voice you hear inside,
people of arrogant being will talk and do,
but love triumphs hate, and
the sweetest revenge is sweet success.

Freedom

I don't know, but I thought after being together for
so long, I knew a little about you and who you are.
I thought you cared for me even the tiniest bit, but I
was wrong.
I don't blame you for finding love where you did
I just thought you were busy loving me.
I won't cry and try to hold on,
I know that you are not what I need.
I made myself believe because we were together so
long that this was heading somewhere.
I made myself think things that were not real
things you wanted me to believe.
Letting go won't be hard because I am free to find
love that is true love that is faithful.
I feel anger for the time I wasted loving a man who
did not deserve my love, that did not deserve my
faith, that did not deserve my tears.
I lost myself loving you and as the freedom to be
myself washes over me,
I laugh for the weight that has lifted off my heart
I laugh for the joy filling my soul, for the light
shining from my eyes, and feel sorrow for the
woman who believes she has your love.

Halafa Parke

Paradise

Waking up to the rising sun
and warm ocean breeze
paradise welcomes me.

Stretching my rested body
a smile on my face
the beauty of this place humbles me.

Sand between my toes, a song in my soul
I found a peace I had yet to know
the beauty of this place seduces as it welcomes
enticing me to spend forever on its rested shores.

Enjoying the comforts of the natives
basking in all the wickedness, they have to offer
laughing until my soul was free.

How freeing to be away from the troubles of
every day, to have a chance to see what life
is about to appreciate the joy of just
being alive, stopping for a moment to laugh
out loud and feel just how wonderful it feels.

To sit and watch the sunset and think of the
one with whom you want to share it all.
To look at life and see what is missing, and
try and find the answers we all seek.
To take some time and just breathe,
to finally realize what we all need,
the one thing we can't live without, love.

I've found love

I've found love, and it has transformed
me into a beautiful bloom.
Now light shines from me like a prism in the sun
hear me laugh, see me smile.
I welcome each day as if it's my last,
love is peace, and it is joy.
It is a journey through tears and fears,
but the rewards are sweet and everlasting.

Love restores our faith and mends our broken hearts
love gives us wings so we can fly once more.
When love embraces us, we embrace the world
love is a source of strength, building confidence.
Love opened up my heart so I could let you in, and
you came in and opened the world up to me.

.

Black and white

Why dream dreams that may never come through?
Why ask questions to which you know there
are no answers forthcoming?
Why cry over a loss when the pain may never end,
why live in the past when we can never go back?

So many questions without answers, but
every day without an end.
For every new love found, so many are lost.
For every life we gain, we rejoice,
for every life that's lost, it's a beginning.

I wonder about tomorrow, but make no promises,
I put so much into today but gain so little.
I've never loved before, but came close to hate,
I watch the rainfall while the sun disappears.
I hear your cries I imagine your pain,
I hear your voice. I see no face.
Today is so much like every day, but
so different from yesterday and
black and white could be twins.

Love is

If love were like the ocean, it would never run dry.
If love were like the sun, it would warm us always,
but love is complicated and always worth the pain.
It breaks us down, but then rebuilds us stronger
it can open doors to such amazing wonders.

Love has me question my choices and shows
me I deserve better.
Love is a teacher that teaches forever
love is a journey of discovery, finding you, finding
me.

Love is a gift that keeps on giving,
it is a promise that is never broken.
Love is a smile from a stranger when your heart is
sad.
It is a rainy day wrapped in your warmth.

It is a song that lifts my spirit when I'm feeling low,
it is laughter that brings light to your eyes,
a smile to your face.
It is in the swaying of the trees and the birds
singing in their midst.

Love is seeing the stars reflected in your eyes,
it is seeing you grow into who you were meant to be.
It is the good times and the bad, and being there
through it all.

Halafa Parke

Love is being true to who I am, accepting my faults,
love is kind, love is forgiving, and love is
understanding.

Too blind to see

I have a question for you, what would you say if I
told you I didn't love you?
Would you call me a fool for not knowing the real
thing or be relieved you won't hurt my feelings when
you walk out on me?
How wrong was I to think that after so long
together, you would come to care even a little about
me, but I won't cry not for something that was never
real.
I gave you more than anyone ever has
but you just couldn't see it.
I can't keep on loving you when you don't know
what love is.
I can't open myself up for any more pain, for any
more loss.
I know you have never felt love
never known genuine tenderness before,
but all you had to do was look into my eyes,
concentrate on my touch, listen to the tone of my
voice, it was all there freely given, but you
were too blind to see a love that was real.

☐

Halafa Parke

Betrayed

I never knew
but always assumed
that when I fell in love, it would be forever.
That the joy that filled my heart would never subside
that I could always look into your eyes and be proud.
You made me ashamed of the word, and the feeling
called love destroyed my faith in trusting my heart
again.
My soul bled from the pain of your betrayal
my heart agonizes.
You were my hero, the only person I could trust and
thought deserving of my love
but you shattered it all for me, destroyed my world.
Will I ever regain what once was?
Will I love or trust again?
How can I when my hurt is so complete.

Look into my eyes

Look into my eyes
tell me what you see
tell me what you feel.

Can you see my misery?
Can you feel my pain?
Your ridicule makes me strong
your laughter strengthens my will
I oppose your hate
confront your vanity.

Look into my eyes
tell me what you see
tell me what you feel.

Can you see the dying
embers of the flower which
once bloomed so beautifully?
Can you feel the agony of its demise?

Look into my eyes
tell me what you see
tell me what you feel.

Can you see the pain that lays dormant?
Can you feel the agony of my emotions?
Look at me, and you will see
all my pain raging through me.

Look into my eyes,

Halafa Parke

tell me what you see
tell me what you feel.

Can you see love?
Can you feel hate?
And if you should say I love you
I shall float way,
look into my eyes.
☐ ☐

Don't speak

The bible says the rich will be rich,
and the poor, poorer.
I have worked so hard and have
nothing to show for it.
The more I work, the less I have,
the more I try, the harder it gets.
The farther I go, the more distance it seems,
I try not to complain, only to keep going.

Love yourself before anyone can love you.
I'm fighting a battle inside one that
seems impossible to win,
but I'll be strong.
Life has never been easy
happiness will be my greatest challenge,
love my greatest triumph.

I want to walk. You tell me to run.
You tell me to run, but I will walk.
I will be, but of my own making
don't try and channel the path I will
take, you'll be disappointed.

I was meek as a child,
respectful as a teen,
tolerant now, but what of tomorrow?
I try not to judge, but
I can't promise I won't.

I can say I love you, but do I really.

Halafa Parke

I can say I love you and then try.
I can say I'll kill you, and then you die.
If I ask you to stay, will you go?
If I ask you to love me, what will you say?

I laugh, but you cry,
I sing you close your ears,
I go for a walk. You want to drive.
I want to die. You choose to live.
I will forever be happy, you forever be sad,
I will be the sun, and you can be the moon,
and we will go our separate ways
for life to me is like death to you, and
death to you is life to me.

How I long to be me

We see things that make us want more than we are
allowed, make us hope, make us dream only to wake
up and find out it's not real.
I hear laughter ringing in my ears, and I wonder
would my reaction to such an incredible sound be
different were it my child instead of a nameless,
faceless one.
Would my heart leap each time I heard that perfect
sound?
Would time stop and leave that moment be?
Would my life be more fulfilled, have a deeper
meaning?
Would I be more than just existing, just barely
making it through each day?
What wonders lie out there for me to find in the eyes
of a child of mine?
What joy abound that I have yet to find?
There is such beauty in my dreams
my reality shattered like pieces of broken glass
life has other plans for me
faith has different dreams
I hadn't known until I heard the baby's laughter
how much I long to be free, how I longed to be me.
☐

Halafa Parke

Love's pain

I use to believe in love and all the candy sweetness
it brought.
I use to believe that no matter what
you faced in a relationship if you have love
you can overcome it all but is love real I find
myself asking my heart has been broken
too many times for it to be, my world come crashing
down on me.
I mean, if love is real, my heart wouldn't ache,
I wouldn't be left wondering where it all went
wrong, I wouldn't be a crumpled mess laying on the
floor waiting for the pieces of my shattered heart
to mend, waiting for the faith I once had in my
ability to tell when someone was being true to me to
return.
I have seen the devastation love can bring, the pain
in the eyes of others who have loved and endured
the pain love often brings, my faith in love is lost
and nothing in the world can make me want to feel
that pain again.

Mom

For all that's good
for all that's bad
for the right, and
for the wrong.
For all the times
you scold me,
for all the tears I shed.
For all the good you taught me,
for all the lessons I learned.
For all the love I know,
for all the love I feel,
for the person I am and
the one I will become.
I thank you for your love
and my love in return.

To give

To give so much to everyone, and
receive so little in return
makes my heart cry.
To be judged so severely, and
punished do harshly
makes me wonder about this life.

To be accused without question,
charged without knowledge
makes me feel sorry for them.

For what they don't know is that purgatory
is behind you, and the way is cleared
for a better day.

One day they will say I should have asked
questions, gather all the facts, and not be
so quick to judge, but it shall be too late,
and you shall be where they will never be.
Attain what they never dreamed, and you
shall be just who you are, the nicest, kindest
person I ever met. Just be you.

Spite

Do what you please,
say what you will,
for I care not what you think.
I woke up this morning,
or did I?
But you see me here,
do you see tears in my eyes?
Oh, but you can't see inside.

Two can play the game of spite,
and I, for one, happens to be very
good at this very game.
I am used to the eyes, the whispers and all,
but here I am, still going strong.
What will happen to me if I let myself be defeated?
Whatever you throw at me, I skillfully avoid.

I am stronger than you seem to think,
more intelligent than I even know.
You can't hurt me with words, thoughts, or
otherwise; that would prove me weak, and I need to
be stronger than you to survive.

☐
☐

Halafa Parke

The heart

Sometimes we get in our own way and
say things we shouldn't have said.
We walk away instead of standing firm and
fighting for what we want.
We blame others for our mistakes instead of being
an adult, and facing what we have done.

Love is never easy.
That's why we fight to keep it strong.
The heart is amazing; if only we let it take the lead
more often, we would find ourselves more in
harmony.
Sometimes we get it wrong and don't know the
words to say, but if you love someone and don't
know what to say, open your heart and let it say
what is to be said, don't try too hard, let things
unfold by themselves you may never know what is
there to be said, but your heart knows.

The heart does not lie and will reveal the love hidden
inside.
Love is such a powerful word; I love you an even
more powerful phrase, and only the heart knows the
words that best describe the feelings of love itself.
☐
☐

I need a real man

You say you love me
you say you want me
tell me how you need me
how good you are at telling me
what you think I want to hear
I don't need pretty words
I don't need false devotion.

You say you're sorry
you promise you'll change
and beg me to stay.
How easily the lies roll off your tongue,
how gullible do you think I am?
A few kisses and an apology
you think it makes everything alright.

You make promises and play games
trying to hold on to something that is no more.
Hoping for something that will never be
I want a man who stands by his words
who will be there when I need him
to be my friend, to be my lover
to be the end of my forever.

□ □

Halafa Parke

My newborn child

I often wondered how it would
feel to love someone completely,
then I felt you move inside me.
When I first held you in my arms
I was overwhelmed by the love I felt.
When I looked into your eyes, eyes that knew me,
when I saw your first smile so pure and so innocent
I knew I would lay down my life for you.
You became my entire world
you became my reason for living
your brought purpose to this world, and
made everything I do worth all the
sacrifices I had to make, all the pain I had to endure.
You are the heart of me, my greatest blessing, the
gift of a lifetime.

You there

I wonder, do you wonder
well, it's like this
no one ever sees the good I do,
do you feel that way?
I bet you do and get this,
everyone always sees the bad.
That makes me want to scream,
don't you? I mean, tell me when I do wrong,
don't jump on me about it.
And don't you hate when they make
a mistake, which is often, they expect
you not to say anything.
What are they thinking?

They expect you to see them as human
in their mistakes, and I ask what am I?
I mean, and listen to this one, you do
all the work, they take all the credit,
but then I'm stupid for I say nothing.
I know you sometimes do too
for its understandable, but
sometimes it just goes too far,
do you know what I mean?

You and I could become good friends, you know,
we understand each other so well.
Ha-ha-ah, oh boy!
Do you ever feel like saying no to a favor,
but then you know you'll feel guilty?
It's not my fault what happened, but

Halafa Parke

I end up carrying the blame, and
they just stand there and look at me,
girl, I tell you.
It seems funny some of the things
that happen, hey you there I'm
talking to you. Oh, forget you.

This fool

You son of a bitch, sleeping in my bed
eating at my table, taking of my body
leading my heart to a place you know
you will never be.
Pretending to care about me all the while
you were loving someone else,
the bastard you are thinking you are playing
me for a fool when I know for a fact that you will
be the one hurt. She doesn't want you.
She is in love with someone else
don't come calling at my door this
fool has suffered you long enough.

Made in the USA
Columbia, SC
22 August 2022

65417473R00057